The Messenger Bag

BY JILLIAN POWELL
ILLUSTRATED BY CHARLOTTE ALDER

Librarian Reviewer
Marci Peschke
Librarian, Dallas Independent School District
MA Education Reading Specialist, Stephen F. Austin State University
Learning Resources Endorsement, Texas Women's University

Reading Consultant
Sherry Klehr
Elementary/Middle School Educator, Edina Public Schools, MN
MA in Education, University of Minnesota

 STONE ARCH BOOKS
Minneapolis   San Diego

First published in the United States in 2008
by Stone Arch Books
151 Good Counsel Drive, P.O. Box 669
Mankato, Minnesota 56002
www.stonearchbooks.com

Originally published in Great Britain in 2006
by Badger Publishing Ltd

Original work copyright © 2006 Badger Publishing Ltd
Text copyright © 2006 Jillian Powell

The right of Jillian Powell to be identified as the author
of this work has been asserted by her in accordance
with the Copyright, Designs and Patent Act 1988.

Library of Congress Cataloging-in-Publication Data
Powell, Jillian.
    [Handbag Wars]
    The Messenger Bag / by Jillian Powell; illustrated by Charlotte
Alder.
    p. cm. — (Keystone books)
    Summary: When Stacey buys an old Kelly handbag at a thrift shop,
it seems to magically supply her with just what she needs.
    ISBN 978-1-4342-0474-5 (library binding)
    ISBN 978-1-4342-0524-7 (paperback)
    [1. Magic—Fiction. 2. Handbags—Fiction. 3. Theater—Fiction.]
I. Alder, Charlotte, ill. II. Title.
PZ7.P87755Me 2008
[Fic]—dc22
        2007028508

1 2 3 4 5 6 13 12 11 10 09 08

Printed in the United States of America

Table of Contents

CHAPTER 1

A New Handbag

"That is so cute!" Stacey said.

"They had it in blue too," Becca said.

"No, pink is perfect," Stacey told her.

Becca held out the bag. "You should get one," she said. "They are so trendy."

Stacey and Becca were crazy about handbags. They had a handbag contest going on.

Right now, Becca was winning. She always had the cutest new bag. She had hundreds of them. But it was easier for her. Her mom worked in a store. She got good deals.

Stacey was losing the contest.

"Is that new?" Becca asked. She looked down at Stacey's bag.

"No. It's the one I got last year, remember?" Stacey said.

"Oh, yes. I remember. They were trendy last year," Becca said.

Becca turned to go. She smiled at Stacey. Then she waved goodbye and headed off with her new pink bag.

Stacey sighed. Her bag was so unstylish.

CHAPTER 2

An Old Handbag

It was Saturday morning. Stacey was working at the thrift store.

"What should I do first?" she asked Rita, the store manager.

"Sort this box of stuff, please, dear," Rita said. She handed Stacey a big box.

Stacey opened the box. It was mostly full of clothes. Then she saw the handbag.

It was black. It was beautiful.

"Hey, Rita. Look at this!" she said.

"Oh! It's a Kelly bag!" Rita said.

"A what?" Stacey asked.

"They were really trendy about fifty years ago," Rita told her. "They named them after Grace Kelly."

Stacey was confused.

Rita said, "She was a beautiful actress who became a princess."

"Oh!" Stacey said. She slid the Kelly bag on her arm. It smelled like leather.

"It is so pretty," she told Rita. "Can I buy it?"

Rita nodded. "No need to put a price tag on it!"

Stacey put some money in the register.

She wanted to show Becca. Becca could never match this one.

At home, Stacey opened the bag and felt inside. There was something in one of the pockets. It was a lipstick, in a gold case. She read the name. It was French. It said, "La Vie en Rose."

CHAPTER 3

A Time and A Place

Becca came over on the way to school. "It's so cool!" she agreed.

"There's red silk inside," Stacey said.

Then she saw something else inside. "That's funny," she said. It was a note. Stacey hadn't seen it before. She read it out loud. "Tuesday the 4th. 5 p.m., Bay Theater."

"Today is Tuesday the 4th," Becca said. "That's spooky!"

"Don't be silly," Stacey said. "It's just an old note.

Still, Bay Theater was on the way home from school.

Stacey got off the bus there after school. There was a crowd waiting outside. She took out the note again.

Then a man pushed her inside the hall. "First door on the left!" the man said to Stacey.

Stacey went where she was told. There were three people sitting at a long table.

"Okay. Take your time," a man said. "Show us what you can do. Sing. Dance. Whatever!"

Stacey couldn't sing, but she could dance.

"Thank you! Do you do any tap dancing?" one of the women asked.

"No," Stacey said. "I can learn fast."

"Write your name down here. We'll be in touch!" the woman said.

CHAPTER 4

The Races

The next day, Stacey went to see Granddad. She told him about the audition at Bay Theater.

Granddad knew she wanted to be a dancer, like her grandma had been. "You should take tap lessons," Granddad said.

"Mom says they cost too much," Stacey said.

"Maybe I can help," Granddad said.

"No way, Granddad!" Stacey knew Granddad wasn't rich.

"Well, why don't we go to the races today?" Granddad said. "Maybe we can win the money!"

Granddad loved horse racing.
He needed some cheering up since
Grandma died. Stacey agreed to go.

When they got there, Granddad
took out ten dollars. They looked at
the list of horses.

Then Stacey saw it: one of the horses
was named La Vie en Rose.

That was it! They had to put the
money on that one.

"That horse never wins!" Granddad
said. But he agreed anyway.

The race began. The crowd began
to yell and cheer. "Where's our horse?"
Stacey asked Granddad.

"Stacey!" Granddad was jumping up
and down. "It's winning! It's winning!
We won!"

It was a big win.

"There's enough here for tap lessons!" Stacey told Granddad. "Thank you, La Vie en Rose!"

CHAPTER 5

A Surprise

The next day, a letter came.

"Mom! I got a part in a new stage show! I'm going to be a dancer!" Stacey yelled, jumping around. "I have to learn tap, and we start rehearsing in six weeks. I have to call Becca."

Stacey went to get her Kelly bag.

She looked inside for her phone. There was a green ticket inside.

That was weird.

It hadn't been there before.

"Mom, did you put this in my bag?" she asked.

Mom shook her head. "It looks like a ticket for dry cleaning," Mom said. "Someone forgot it, I guess."

After school, Stacey went into town. The ticket had a store's name on it. She found the store and went inside.

The woman in the store took the ticket. She looked at the number and went into the back of the shop. Then she came out with a box.

"They're paid for," she told Stacey.

Stacey stepped outside. She opened the box and gasped.

It was a pair of tap shoes, and they were her size.

Stacey shivered. This was starting to get weird.

CHAPTER 6

The Scent of Success

The weeks flew by. Stacey loved her tap dance class. She loved the show even more. It was so much fun. She had even made new friends.

She always took her Kelly bag out when she went shopping with Becca. Becca had a new bag every time.

Stacey wasn't jealous of her anymore. Becca was always asking about the show.

Soon it was the opening night. The cast had a party. Stacey dressed up and took her Kelly bag. She was showing it to one of her new friends when she found something inside. It was a bottle of perfume.

She showed Mom when she got home. "It looks pretty old," Mom said. "Ask Granddad if he knows what it is."

Stacey took the bottle of perfume to Granddad's house.

Granddad looked at the bottle. He closed his eyes and sniffed.

Then he smiled. "New York!" he said. "It's called New York. Your grandma used to wear that. She loved it. Sometimes she put too much on."

That night, Stacey put the bottle beside her bed. The moon shone on its silver top. Stacey dreamed about the bright lights of New York City.

Good News

The show went on for twelve weeks. It was hard work, but Stacey loved it. It got great reviews. The cast got their picture in the paper.

Granddad had seen the show six times. "Your grandma would have been so proud," he told Stacey.

Granddad was there when Stacey heard the news. After a Saturday show, the director called the cast together.

"Guys, I have some news for you,"
he told them. "Pack your bags. We're
going to do a show in New York City!"

Everyone in the cast cheered and
clapped, but Stacey was quiet. She
looked across at Granddad. He winked
and smiled at her. Stacey knew he was
thinking about the perfume, too.

CHAPTER 8

A Discovery

Becca came over the next day. "I have something for you!" she told Stacey. "It's for good luck."

Stacey opened it. It was a red bag. "It's so trendy," Becca told her. "The girls in New York are really cool. You can't take your old bag."

Stacey looked down at her Kelly bag. "Thanks," she told Becca. "I'll call you when I get there and tell you all about it."

Later, Granddad came over to say goodbye to Stacey. "Are you all packed?" he asked.

Stacey nodded.

"You will call me, won't you? Got your phone?" Granddad asked.

Stacey nodded again and held up her bag. Granddad was suddenly silent. He was staring at the handbag.

"Granddad?" Stacey asked.

"That bag of yours," Granddad said slowly. "It's just like one your grandma had, years ago."

Stacey felt a shiver.

"What happened to Grandma's?" she asked Granddad.

"Well, it went to the thrift store with all her other things," Granddad said.

Stacey hugged the bag. She had to take it with her to New York. It was like having Grandma with her, sending her messages. And, after all, Stacey never knew where the bag would take her next!

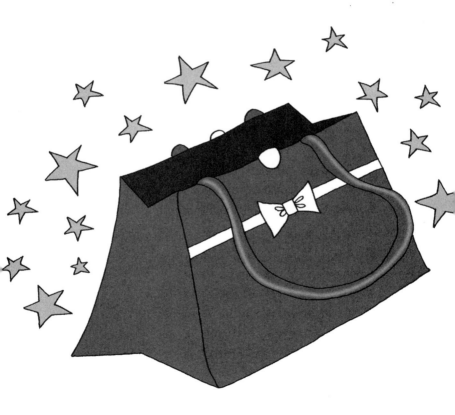

About the Author

Jillian Powell started writing when she was very young. She loved having a giant pad of paper and some pens or crayons in front of her. She made up newspaper stories about jewel thieves and spies. Jillian's parents still have her early stories, complete with crayon illustrations!

About the Illustrator

Charlotte Alder has always worked in creative environments, but illustrating children's books is her favorite job. She says that her inspiration and best critics of her children's books are her nieces and nephews, who range in age from 3 to 14. She always gets honest answers from them! Charlotte lives in Devon, England, and she says, "For fresh ideas all I need to do is look out of my window or take a walk along the beach. It always seems to work!"

Glossary

audition (aw-DISH-uhn)—a short performance to see if a person gets a part in a show

director (duh-REK-tur)—the person in charge of making a play, show, or movie

handbag (HAND-bag)—a bag in which a woman carries her wallet and other things

leather (LETH-ur)—animal skin that is treated with chemicals and used to make goods

register (REJ-uh-stur)—a cash register is a machine that holds and counts money

rehearsing (ri-HURS-sing)—practicing

reviews (ri-VYOOZ)—opinions about a show or movie

spooky (SPOO-kee)—creepy or weird

tap dancing (TAP DANSS-ing)—a form of dance using special shoes that make clicking sounds

thrift store (THRIHFT STOR)—a store that sells used goods

trendy (TREN-dee)—fashionable, cool

unstylish (un-STY-lish)—not fashionable

Discussion Questions

1. After she got a new bag, strange things started happening to Stacey. Can you explain why? Talk about different reasons the strange things might have happened.

2. Stacey knows that her granddad misses her grandmother a lot. What are some ways to remember people who aren't with you anymore? Talk about it.

3. Do you think Stacey's feelings were hurt when Becca told her she shouldn't take her Kelly bag to New York? What should Stacey have said? How would you have handled it?

Writing Prompts

1. Stacey and Becca have a very competitive friendship. Do you think that's good or bad? Write a few paragraphs that explain what you think about Stacey and Becca's friendship.

2. At the end of this book, Stacey is getting ready to leave for New York City. What do you think happens once she gets there? Write another chapter that begins when Stacey gets to New York!

3. In this book, Stacey wants to take tap dancing lessons. What is something you'd like to learn? Write about the thing you'd like to learn, and explain why.

Also by Jillian Powell

Sleepwalker

Weird things have happened since Josh moved in with his new stepbrother. Tom begins to sleepwalk! Josh believes his stepbrother is playing tricks on him. But one night, the sleepwalking adventure turns to sudden horror!

Roller Coaster

Three friends are not old enough to ride on the Devil Dipper roller coaster. But they won't let silly rules stop them. When the park closes, they will sneak onto the ride. Will it be the ride of their lives . . . or will it be the last ride they ever take?

Other Books in This Set

Self Defender
by Jane West

Tess's new school seems okay, until a spiteful bully makes her school life miserable. Tess has to learn a new way to defend herself. Then she must wait until the moment that she can use her new skills!

Warning from the Waves
by Justine Smith

Tara loves living by the ocean. One day, she meets a strange boy underwater. He seems to have an important message for Tara. She doesn't know what it means. What is the boy's warning?

Internet Sites

Do you want to know more about subjects
related to this book? Or are you interested
in learning about other topics? Then check
out FactHound, a fun, easy way to find
Internet sites.

Our investigative staff has already sniffed out
great sites for you!

Here's how to use FactHound:

1. Visit *www.facthound.com*

2. Select your grade level.

3. To learn more about subjects related
   to this book, type in the book's ISBN number:
   9781434204745.

4. Click the **Fetch It** button.

FactHound will fetch the best Internet sites
for you!

DATE DUE

SEP 09			
SEP 10			
SEP 16			
OCT 0 7 2009			
NOV 1 2 2009			
NOV 3 0 2009			
DEC 0 2 2009			
SEP 2 1 2010			
NOV 2 0 2010			